GREEN WILMA
FROG IN SPACE

TEDD ARNOLD

SCHOLASTIC INC.
New York Toronto London Auckland
Sydney Mexico City New Delhi Hong Kong

Specially for
Carmen and Morgan

ISBN 978-0-545-26200-2

12 11 10 9 8 7 6 5 4 3 2 1   11 12 13 14 15/0

Printed in the U.S.A.   40

First Scholastic printing, May 2010

Design by Nancy R. Leo-Kelly
Text set in ITC Cheltenham
The artwork was prepared using color pencils and watercolor washes.

One morning Wilma woke to hear
a buzzing in the sky.

She hopped into the air to catch
a tasty little fly.

An alien family landed,
needing water for their ship.

An alien child came out to play.
He took a little dip.

Finally, Green Wilma's breakfast
landed on the ground.

Carefully she crept up, trying
not to make a sound.

Suddenly the spaceship plucked her
up into the air.

It pulled her in, and then it rose
and flew away from there.

Poor Wilma at the window watched
her little pond retreat.
But then she heard her favorite words:

"I fixed your favorite: Martian bugs,"
the alien mother said.

"But you can't eat until I take
this helmet off your head.

"It must have been the pond water
that turned our Blooger green.

Just get some rest while we turn on
the Health-O-Mat machine."

Robot doctors tried to find out
what the problem was.

And only Wilma noticed a
familiar little buzz.

She chased it all around the room

and out into the ship.

She hopped across the flight controls

and things began to tip.

The spaceship went from warp speed
into boogie-woogie drive.

It bounced off planets, circled stars,
then fell into a dive.

Green Wilma grabbed the nearest thing
and held on to it tight.
The ship flew back the way it came.
Her home rose into sight.

Back at Miller's Pond, poor Blooger
hid inside a tree.
But when he heard a sound he knew,
he hopped outside to see.

Overhead, the aliens booted
Wilma out the door.

They picked up little Blooger and
departed with a roar.

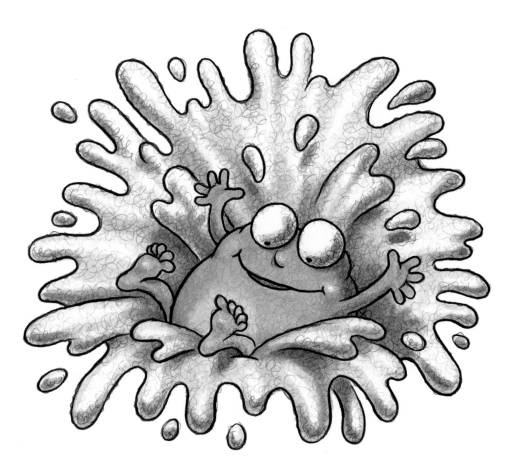

Green Wilma felt quite certain it
had all been just a dream.

No way had she gone up in space
—as real as it might seem!

But what, exactly, was this thing
that shot a pretty beam?